# RUDOLPH
## The Red-Nosed Reindeer

By BARBARA SHOOK HAZEN

*Adapted from the story by*
ROBERT L. MAY

A GOLDEN BOOK • NEW YORK
Western Publishing Company, Inc., Racine, Wisconsin 53404

Here is a delightful version of the tale of Rudolph, the red-nosed
reindeer—the little reindeer so well known in song and story.
Accompanied by Richard Scarry's fresh, imaginative illustrations, this
Golden Book will bring joy to every Christmas stocking. Any material
from the song RUDOLPH THE RED-NOSED REINDEER, copyright
MCMIL by St. Nicholas Music, Inc., is used in this book by permission
of the copyright proprietor.

Once there was a reindeer named Rudolph, who lived at the North Pole, in Toyland.

Rudolph was younger and smaller than the other reindeer there. They all had proud, tall antlers. Rudolph's antlers were only tiny stubs.

Worst of all, Rudolph had a nose that was big and bright red. It was so red it glowed in the dark.

Poor Rudolph! He wanted to be like the other reindeer in Toyland. Oh, to have a small, brown nose, instead of a big, bright, red one!

The other reindeer made fun of Rudolph and called him names.

"Rudolph, the red-nosed reindeer," they teased over and over again until tears glistened on Rudolph's large red nose.

They kicked up snowballs with their tiny hoofs and covered Rudolph with a blanket of white, fluffy snow.

Sometimes the other reindeer made a circle around Rudolph and sang:

*"Red-nose, red-nose,*
*A funny sight!*
*Big as an apple,*
*And twice as bright!"*

All the reindeer loved to play games. They played tree tag and snow slide and tumble bones.

But Rudolph was never asked to play. He stood behind a pine tree and watched. He was very lonely.

Rudolph couldn't even play hide-and-seek with the rabbits. His glowing red nose gave him away every time.

Before Christmas Eve, Santa's elves posted a sign on the gate to Toyland.

"Santa's Team-choosing Time," the sign said.

All the reindeer were asked to line up at eight o'clock in the meadow. Santa Claus was coming to choose the team that would deliver presents to every good little boy and girl in the world.

The reindeer fairly danced with excitement when they heard the news. They pranced, and tossed their antlers, and pawed the snowy ground with their hoofs.

Each reindeer hoped he would be chosen to guide Santa's sleigh. It was the greatest honor a reindeer could ever have.

Rudolph sighed. He was ashamed to have Santa see his bright red nose. So he decided to hide.

In the meadow all the reindeer in Toyland, except Rudolph, stood in a line while Santa inspected them. Santa chose carefully—only the fastest, the strongest, and the best reindeer would do.

"I think Dasher will be fine. He's the biggest reindeer," said Santa.

"Dasher," wrote his elf assistant in a big book.

"And Dancer is the strongest," said Santa, pulling his beard.

"Dancer," wrote the elf.

"Ho! Ho! Let's see," continued Santa. "Here's Prancer and here's Vixen. They make the smoothest landings on rooftops.

"Comet is the fastest, and Cupid is the most sure-footed," said Santa. "I pick them.

"And last," said Santa, "I choose Donder and Blitzen. They're best at twisting over tree tops and skimming over telephone poles."

The reindeer in Santa's team were very happy. They rubbed noses. They danced and clinked their antlers together.

Even the reindeer who weren't chosen were given good jobs. One was to try out electric trains. Another was to cuddle Christmas kittens.

The only reindeer without a job was Rudolph. He wanted to help, but he knew he would be laughed at.

At last it was Christmas Eve. Santa and his elves were busy packing the sleigh.

"I don't care if they do make fun of me," said Rudolph suddenly. "I want to help, too! I'll bring Santa's team a pail of nice cool water," he decided. "They'll get thirsty on their long journey."

The night was bitter cold and a terrible fog covered all the earth.

Santa's elves kept bumping into each other as they hitched up the team. They could hardly see as they put on each bright red harness and tied each jingle bell.

To make matters worse, Dasher and Dancer were fighting over who was to be lead reindeer.

"I was chosen first!" said Dasher, stamping angrily.

"But you always trip over the moon!" said Dancer, kicking a fallen star.

Even Santa was cross. "We'll never get there if you two don't stop quarreling," he said. "And where is my Christmas list? Dash it all! I can't see a thing in this fog!"

Just then a soft red glow lit up the snow.

"Thank goodness," said Santa, suddenly jolly again.
"I've found my list. Ho! Ho! I must have tucked it in
my belt.

"Who brought this fine lantern?" asked Santa. "I must take it with me. Why, I can see perfectly now."

"It's not a lantern," said Rudolph, trembling. "The light comes from my . . . my nose."

"Rudolph, the red-nosed reindeer!" said Santa. "I'm certainly glad to see you. Your light will guide my sleigh tonight. I appoint you head of my team and number one reindeer in all the world!"

Rudolph held his head high. Proudly he pranced to the front of the team.

All the other reindeer bowed. Donder and Dancer helped Rudolph put on his harness, and Cupid gave him a beautiful sprig of holly berries.

Then down, down through the clouds and over the sleeping houses, Santa and his team flew on that foggy Christmas Eve.

And leading the whole procession was Rudolph, the red-nosed reindeer!

So if you see a soft glow in the sky on Christmas Eve, you can be sure that Rudolph, "the most famous reindeer of all," is very near.